IT'S WINGMAN!

Donald held his breath. The shining figure looked stern and friendly at once. Suddenly, with a rush of feathers, the figure jumped off the beam. Donald felt his heart thump once, hard.

He looked down over the side of the bridge. The man in armor was gone. He looked up and saw something like a big gray bird disappear, flying into the sun.

Was it really Wingman?

"[Donald's] story is told with such absolute conviction that it's easy to believe it's 'mostly true.' You might also say that this is a wonderfully internalized report on the growth of creative vision . . . or, more simply, that Donald is an artist for sure."

—*Kirkus Reviews* (starred review)

"A decidedly different, easy-to-read story which effectively deals with how fantasy provides a protective covering from hurts and prejudices."

—*School Library Journal* (starred review)

WINGMAN

Written and illustrated by
DANIEL PINKWATER

A BANTAM SKYLARK BOOK ®
NEW YORK • TORONTO • LONDON • SYDNEY • AUCKLAND

This edition contains the complete text
of the original hardcover edition.
NOT ONE WORD HAS BEEN OMITTED.

RL 3, 007-010

WINGMAN

A Bantam Skylark Book / published by arrangement with the author

PRINTING HISTORY
Dodd, Mead edition published 1975
Dell Yearling edition published 1976
Bantam edition / January 1992

Bantam Books are published by Bantam Books, a division of Ban-
tam Doubleday Dell Publishing Group, Inc. Its trademark, consist-
ing of the words ''Bantam Books'' and the portrayal of a rooster, is
Registered in U.S. Patent and Trademark Office and in other coun-
tries. Marca Registrada. Bantam Books, 666 Fifth Avenue, New
York, New York 10103.

For Mr. Yee and Mr. Yee

献呈

余少老先生

平和德

At school he was Donald Chen, but at home he was Chen Chi-Wing or Ah-Wing. Although he was born in New York, he didn't know any English before he went to school. He had been going to school for a while now, and he knew English. Sometimes he wasn't sure if he was Donald or Wing. He was sure that it was cold at home in winter and cold at school. He was sure he was the poorest kid in class. He was sure he was the only Chinese kid in Public School 132.

The cold didn't bother him. He didn't care how cold it got. He never wore a coat. Every day he went to school in the fresh white shirt his father washed and ironed for him the night before. He had a coat though. He wore it once, when the rumor spread that he didn't have one. He just wore it one day, and made sure everybody saw it. After that he didn't wear it anymore because the cold didn't bother him.

When he was a very little kid, before he could remember, the whole family was together and they lived in Chinatown. He couldn't remember anything about it. Now they lived in Washington Heights, and their mother was in the hospital, and they were poor, and he was the only Chinese kid in school. Sometimes his father took him to Chinatown. It was always warm there. There were lots of people in the streets, and there were good smells from restaurant kitchens. He would help his father get the groceries, and wait at the newsstand while his father talked to his friends, and played a game of Mah-Jongg. The newsstand belonged to an old guy called Oi-Lai Bok. Lai would talk to him, and let him read comics. Lai called him Ah-Wing.

Wing lived behind his father's laundry with his little brother and sister. He ate and slept there, and he kept his comic books there in a lot of old wooden boxes. He got comics with money he made collecting bottles and helping in the laundry. He had over two thousand of them. It had taken a long time to get them, and he worked very hard for the money. But they were very important, so he didn't mind working hard.

He had always loved comic books. He couldn't remember when they hadn't been a part of his life. They were the best part of his life. He could remember when his family had been thrown out by the landlord. It had happened twice before they came to the laundry. All their beds and chairs and clothing, and Wing's comic books, were carried out and

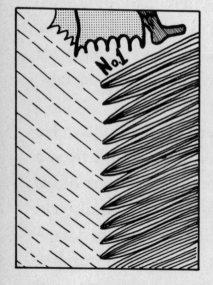

left in the street. Wing stayed with the furniture and his brother and sister while his father went to find someone to help them get a place to live. Reading about Hawkman, and Captain Marvel, and Mr. Scarlet helped him not to worry about things. Once he walked a hundred and twenty-four blocks because he had spent his subway fare on an old Flash comic. He never minded working hard when something was really important.

When he went to school he was Donald, and nothing very good ever happened to him there. He wouldn't have gone at all, but his father wanted him to go. He liked to do the things his father wanted. When he was little, it seemed to him that his father was always carrying him. When he remembered being little, he remembered being carried by his father. He had begun to help his father, ironing handkerchiefs, when he was four years old. When he was five, he began to deliver shirts. His father always gave him work to do, but somehow he always made him like it. When he helped his father in the laundry, sometimes he felt as if his father were carrying him again. His father wanted him to go to school, so he went to school.

School had not been so bad at first. Then everybody found out about how poor Donald Chen was. On the last day of school before Thanksgiving, his teacher, Miss Spinrad, had five baskets of food next to her desk. She explained to the class that some children were very unfortunate, and that we should all be kind to them. The way she talked made Donald Chen feel very sorry for those children. He wished he had known about the baskets before, so he could have brought some comic books to put in them. Then Miss Spinrad called out the names of the five poor children who were going to get the baskets. Donald Chen did not hear the teacher call his name. When he looked up, she was standing in front of his desk. She was holding the basket. It was for him. Donald wanted to say no, but he couldn't say anything. Everybody was looking at him.

Miss Spinrad put the basket on his desk, and he took it home.

That night he saw his father cry. He also saw him jump up and down on a turkey, and throw a lot of groceries and cans of stuff into the garbage. Donald didn't go back to school after Thanksgiving. His father didn't know anything about it.

Donald had a schoolbag. Every morning he would fill it with comic books. Then he would start out for school, but he would turn right a block before the school and head for the river. It was only a few blocks, across Broadway, across Fort Washington Avenue, then down a little street to a footbridge across the Henry Hudson Parkway.

When Donald Chen, Chen Chi-Wing, crossed that footbridge, he entered a little park. There were trees there; the river flowed past, with the wild jungles of New Jersey on the other side. Stretching over everything, so big that he couldn't see the whole thing at once, was the George Washington Bridge.

He knew how to climb the bridge. No other kid he knew was able to do it. The only hard part, really, was scrambling up the bottom part, which was like a wall. Once he got to the big steel beams, it was easy to go from one to the other. With his schoolbag hanging from his belt, he climbed. The steel beams, that looked like spider webs from the little park below the bridge, were big enough to walk on. They slanted up, meeting other beams—roads leading to roads.

He worked his way up to the place where the bridge curves out over the river. He could hear the cars and trucks rumbling over his head. The river flowed slowly beneath him, and boats passed underneath. Pigeons fluttered and sea gulls glided beneath and about him, but he didn't pay much attention. He just checked these things when he arrived

in the morning to make sure everything was still the same. Then he would open his schoolbag.

Donald read comic books all day. He read *Skywolf*, *Captain Marvel*, *Spy Smasher*, and *Plastic Man*. He read *Batman*, *Airboy*, *The Spirit*, and *Superman*. They were real people. They were strong. Everybody respected them. Crooks were afraid of them.

The steel beams of the bridge were made in the shape of a letter H. There was room for Donald to sit inside the H, and when he lay on his stomach, nobody could see him. As he read the comics, the rumbling of the cars on the bridge sounded farther away, and after a while it would fade out, and Donald would read his comics in silence.

In the afternoon, Donald would leave the bridge. It always made him sad to realize that school would be letting out, and it was time to go home. As he crossed the little foot-bridge over the highway, his feet felt heavy, as though he were tired. When he got home, his father would give him a bowl of vegetable soup, and Donald would do some work in the laundry. His father never caught on that Donald was not going to school.

Donald went to the bridge for a long time. It was getting to be real winter. It snowed a couple of times, but Donald never minded the cold. He put a few comic books under him, and was very comfortable.

When Donald met Wingman, he met him on the bridge. Donald looked up from the Aquaman story he was reading, and there was someone standing over him, legs apart, balancing on the edges of the beam. He had steel armor that covered his body, his arms and legs were bare, and he carried a long sword. On his head he wore a strange pointed helmet, and over his shoulders a cape made of gray feathers. It looked like a pair of wings. He seemed to shine all over. He was Chinese.

Donald held his breath. The shining figure looked stern and friendly at once. Suddenly, with a rush of feathers, the figure jumped off the beam. Donald felt his heart thump once, hard. He realized all at once that it was very high up and dangerous on the bridge; he had never thought about it before. At the same moment, he looked down over the side. The man in armor was gone. Donald knew he could not have fallen all that way at once. He looked up and saw something like a big gray bird disappear, flying into the sun.

Donald thought about what he had seen. It seemed that the winged man had just lighted on his particular beam by accident, as pigeons sometimes did, not knowing Donald was there. And just as the pigeons did, he had flown away when Donald had looked at him. Donald decided to be careful not to look at him if he came back. That way, maybe he would stay.

Donald was too excited to read anymore. Usually he could read comics anytime. He even read comics the two times his family had been kicked out of their apartment. He read comics the day his mother went to the hospital. But Wingman's appearance excited him. He had never seen anything like him outside a comic book. Now he was impatient with the stories, and the colors looked dull.

Donald stopped reading and looked out over the river. The sky was blue and clear. A tugboat in the distance made puffs of white smoke. Sea gulls soared and dived, calling to one another. Donald noticed that his nose was running. He thought he might bring his jacket the next day.

Donald didn't see Wingman again that day. He thought about him. He remembered every tiny moment. Sometimes he remembered so clearly that he could almost see him. Almost, but not quite. At night he dreamed Wingman's appearance again and again.

The next day Donald climbed to his beam and opened his schoolbag. *Police Comics Number 58: Plastic Man Meets the Green Terror*; but he didn't really read. He just turned the pages and waited for Wingman. He went through comic after comic, waiting. Then he got involved in a Captain Marvel story. Mr. Mind, a tiny worm in a general's uniform, was the head of a gang called "Mr. Mind's Monster Society of Evil," and Captain Marvel was trying to stop them from stealing two magical black pearls. As Donald read, the bridge noises faded away and things became silent.

In the middle of a fight between Captain Marvel and Captain Nazi, Donald realized that Wingman was there. Donald remembered not to look at him. He saw Wingman's feet balanced on the edges of the beam, and went back to his comic book, pretending to read, turning the pages slowly.

Donald's heart was pounding. As he turned the pages of comic after comic, he would glance up and see the feet. He wanted to look at Wingman, but he was afraid of startling him. Then Wingman sat down. There was a rustle of feathers, and Donald knew that Wingman was sitting across the beam from him, his feet dangling toward the

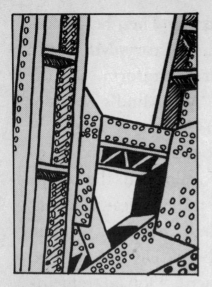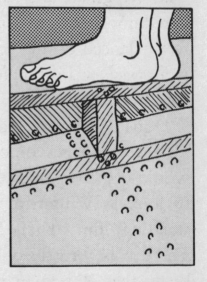

river. Donald looked up slowly. He took in every detail, the sword, the armor, the cape of gray feathers, Wingman's face.

Wingman looked at Donald, smiled, and pushed himself off the beam. Donald looked down and saw Wingman falling, wrapped in his cape. He held his breath. Then the cape unfolded into two gray wings, and Wingman skimmed just above the river, like a sea gull. Then he soared up in a great loop backward, over the bridge. Donald turned and saw him coming from the other side, right toward Donald's beam. As he approached, Wingman gathered his cape around him and hurtled right past Donald like a bullet. Then he spread his cape, and tilted his wings from side to side as though he were waving as he flew away, disappearing among the tall buildings of Manhattan.

Donald felt very happy. He felt as though he were flying too. He didn't read any more comics that day. He sat on the bridge and remembered how Wingman looked flying over the river.

Donald put some sandwiches in his schoolbag in the morning. He went to the bridge and waited for Wingman. Once again he turned the pages of a comic book, not paying attention. Once again he got caught up in a story, this time about Plastic Man, caught by the police for a crime he did not commit. The bridge became silent as Donald read.

When Donald looked up, Wingman was there, sitting across the beam as he had the day before. He was looking out over the river, not noticing Donald. Donald sat for a long time looking at Wingman. Neither of them moved. Wingman appeared to be watching something too far away for Donald to see. Hours passed. Donald was content to study Wingman's cape, sword, and armor. The bridge was silent. Wingman was more interesting than any comic. Wingman never moved. Even the river seemed to be standing still.

Then Donald felt a start, as though he had just come awake, although he hadn't been sleeping. The bridge began to roar with traffic, the river began to move. Donald reached into his schoolbag and took out two sandwiches, salami and peanut butter combination. He put one on the beam next to Wingman and waited to see what would happen. Wingman didn't move. He was still watching something far away. Donald held his own sandwich in his hand and waited.

Still looking into the distance, Wingman reached for the sandwich beside him. He held it in his hand and gave a strange cry. Donald jumped; his hair stood up. Wingman gave the call again, a sad sound that came from high up in his nose. It made Donald's skin tingle.

Wingman's eyes lifted. Donald looked out over the river and saw a big bird flying toward them fast. Very fast. As Donald looked, it got bigger and bigger; then it was right before them. It was as big as Donald himself. Its feathers were gray like those in Wingman's cape. Its beak was black and hooked and sharp. An eagle! It landed between Donald and Wingman. Wingman unwrapped his sandwich and gave half to the bird. Then he took a bite from the other half, and looked at Donald. Donald gave half his sandwich to the bird too. It swallowed it in one gulp after shaking it in its beak. Donald and Wingman smiled at each other and ate their sandwiches.

For the rest of the afternoon, Donald and Wingman sat on the beam in the sunshine. The eagle practiced tightrope walking up and down the edge of the beam between them, sometimes spreading its wings to keep its balance. When it was time to go home, Donald smiled good-by to Wingman and climbed down the bridge. When he reached the bottom, he looked up. He could just see Wingman sitting on the beam. The eagle was flying in circles, under and over the bridge and making piercing cries again and again.

When Donald got home, his uncle Li-Noon was there. He was cooking. Whenever Uncle Noon came they had a feast. He had brought roast pork and lo mein noodles from Chinatown, and big oranges and dry sweet cakes. He also brought a little bottle of whiskey, and he and Donald's father each had a drink out of little glasses. Donald's father ironed in the laundry and Uncle Noon cut up vegetables in the kitchen, and they shouted to each other from room to room, talking Chinese too fast for the children to understand.

At supper Uncle Noon gave presents to the children. Wing's sister got crayons, his little brother got a puzzle made of bent nails, and Donald got lucky money in a red envelope, and a comic book. It was one he had, but he could trade it.

Before he went to bed, Donald tried to draw a picture of Wingman and the eagle. He used his sister's new crayons. He put it in his schoolbag to show Wingman the next day.

In the morning the truant officer caught him. A big man in a linty black suit was waiting for him in the laundry when he woke up. Donald's father kept his back to Donald. Donald knew he was angry. When his father got mad, he would turn his back, and it was worse than anything. He never hit the children. Turning his back to them was much worse.

The truant officer put his hand on Donald's shoulder. Donald began to cry, not because of the truant officer, but because his father was ashamed of him. He wanted to tell his father about how bad it was in school, about the bridge, and Wingman and the eagle, but it was no good. He had fooled his father, and that was the worst thing he could do to him. The truant officer said something to Donald. Donald couldn't hear it. He was crying and all he could see through the tears were his father's shoulders working as he folded shirts.

The truant officer was Mr. Bean, and he wasn't a bad guy. He tried to be nice to Donald. He kept his hand on Donald's shoulder as they walked in the street. Donald supposed it was to keep him from running away, but it felt friendly. He took Donald into the Bickford's Cafeteria on Broadway and bought him breakfast.

"You're not in such bad trouble, kid," Mr. Bean said. "I'd like to know why you were cutting school. Maybe it's a problem I can help you with."

Donald stared at his tray. He was still feeling bad about his father. He wondered if it would be right to tell Mr. Bean about Wingman, and afternoons on the bridge.

"Why aren't you eating your oatmeal?" Mr. Bean asked.

So that was what the gooey stuff was! Donald had never tasted oatmeal. He didn't feel like tasting it now. It didn't look very inviting.

"It's good for you," Mr. Bean said.

Donald tried to pick from among his good reasons for not eating the stuff. "It'll make me sick."

"Now you eat that!" Mr. Bean said. He meant it. Donald began to eat the oatmeal. He had a glimpse of the sad hopeless expression on Mr. Bean's face as he vomited on the cafeteria table.

Donald was told to wait alone in a room next to the office, when they got to school. There was nothing in the room but some chairs around the walls and a noisy clock.

The window was frosted so he couldn't see out, and it had wire fencing on the outside. "Like a jail," he thought. A pigeon was fluttering against the wires. Donald could see its shadow, hazy against the frosted glass. He felt uncomfortable. He wished he had brought some comics. He sat on one of the chairs and waited. He waited for an hour and twenty minutes. The clock ticked. Donald tried to think about Wingman. He would be on the bridge now. Donald tried to imagine that he was there too. It didn't work. The loud ticking kept him from imagining.

The door opened and Mr. Frieda came in. Mr. Frieda was the one they sent you to when you got in trouble. Donald had met him before. Mr. Frieda wore wire eyeglasses that slid down his nose. Whenever they slid down, he would push them back with his middle finger. When he did this, he would stick his little red tongue out. The kids made fun of him behind his back, but he wasn't funny when you met him.

"The fat is in the fire now, boy. The fat is in the fire. You get that, John Chinaman?" Mr. Frieda always wore the same necktie; the knot was black and shiny. "We don't expect much from your kind, but we expect you to be here every day. You understand, boy?"

Donald wished he had a sword like Wingman's.

"You savvy?"

Swish, the sword would go, and cut Mr. Frieda in two. "Yes, Mr. Frieda," Donald said.

"Next time you catch it, Charlie Chan," Mr. Frieda said. Donald wasn't going to be punished; he had cut school day after day, but Mr. Frieda didn't think he was worth bothering about.

Donald was sent back to his class. It was the last day of school before Christmas vacation. Donald had been away almost a month. The class was having its Christmas party. Donald had to sit in a chair in the corner wearing a sign that said TRUANT. He didn't even get to face the wall, but had to watch the other kids playing games and eating cake.

Donald walked home from school very slowly. His feet felt as though they each weighed a hundred pounds. He thought of going to the bridge after school to see if Wingman was still there, but he felt too sad and tired to climb.

Donald walked into the laundry. "The roast duck man came today," his father said. His father didn't stay mad. The roast duck man was someone who brought such things as lop cheong, pork sausage, roast duck, and fresh bok choy from Chinatown. He stopped at all the laundries. Donald was glad he had come that particular day; the roast duck made him feel a little better.

Donald's father was looking at him. "Ah-Wing, some people are not very nice to us. Probably you have trouble with some people, but I want you to go to school just the same. When you get older you can punch them in the nose."

All of a sudden Donald didn't feel so bad. It didn't matter so much about throwing up in the cafeteria, and Mr. Frieda with his dirty necktie, and having to sit in the corner during the class party. He finished his roast duck, and helped his father wrap ironed shirts. His father was singing a song he liked, "I don't want her, you can have her, she's too fat for me," and Donald sang with him.

*D*onald didn't feel altogether better about all that had happened. That night he had a bad dream. He dreamed he was walking toward the laundry late at night. Just before he reached the door, Frankenstein, Dracula, and the Wolfman jumped out of the shadows and began to chase him up St. Nicholas Avenue. There is a steep hill on St. Nicholas Avenue, and in the dream it turned into a cliff just as Donald reached the top. There he was, stuck between jumping and getting caught. Then he woke up. The dream worried him. It made him think of Mr. Bean, Mr. Frieda, and Miss Spinrad.

There was one good thing: there was no school for ten days. He could go to the bridge every day. The bridge was cold and gray. A little wet snow was falling, blowing about the girders. It made them slippery and hard to climb. Donald felt tired. The day was foggy, and he felt foggy in his head, too. When he got to his perch, the fog had hidden the city. He couldn't see the water below. Donald huddled on the beam. The comic he tried to read was getting soggy, so he put it away and just sat, looking out into the pearly gray fog.

He thought about the trouble he'd gotten into at school. He felt bad about disappointing his father, he felt bad about being embarrassed, and about the nasty things Mr. Frieda had said. The worst thing, the thing that made him feel heavy all over, was the realization that now he was going to have to go to that rotten school every day.

Donald tried to think about Wingman. He could not remember what he looked like. Probably he had made him up. The noise from the cars and trucks overhead was a constant drumming. It felt to Donald as though it was coming from inside his head. He sat there for a long time, crying.

Wingman was not real. Comics were a waste of time. Donald was just what the kids called him in the schoolyard, a dumb chinky Chinaman. The same kids made fun of his father. They called him chink too, and ran away. They didn't run away from Donald; he ran away from them. He began to feel the same way he felt when he woke up from the dream about Frankenstein, Dracula, and the Wolfman.

Suddenly Donald realized that he wasn't going to be able to climb down. The bridge was starting to get icy—and, worse, he was scared. He couldn't move. He was like a cat stuck in a tree. All he could do was shiver and think about how high he was. Donald studied the lumpy gray paint on the steel beam. He saw every crack and wrinkle and speck of soot. He watched the snowflakes land and melt and freeze. He couldn't hear the traffic noise. He was bent over, staring at a little patch of paint, and he couldn't straighten up, or even move his eyes. The wrinkled paint made mountains and valleys and rivers and towns. He watched the little map of bridge paint change from gray to red to green.

Green. There were green fields beneath him. The air was not so cold, and there was no more snow. A smooth strong arm was around his waist, and Donald could hear the faint rustle of feathers. Wingman was real! He was carrying Donald, and they were flying.

Donald liked it. He watched the country-side pass beneath them. Now and then a surge of warm air would rise, lifting them straight up. Donald felt perfectly comfortable. He felt as though he could almost fly by himself, without Wingman's help.

The eagle was with them, flying in circles to keep from getting too far ahead. Wingman flew so slowly that they seemed to be hanging still sometimes. Donald felt good. He felt that he was where he belonged. Even the countryside looked familiar to him, although he knew he had never seen it before.

It didn't look like New Jersey. There were strangely shaped hills, and little clusters of houses with roofs made of straw. Groups of people—men, women, and children—were working in the fields. They wore round hats, the kind Donald had seen in shop windows in Chinatown. No one looked up to be amazed at the strange sight of winged man, boy, and eagle passing silently above them.

Donald knew that China was very far from New York. His father had told him that it was so far away that once you left, it was impossible to go back. But this was China for sure.

The houses were getting more numerous and closer together now. Some of them had roofs of wood or tile, and there were lots of people and animals on the roads. They were coming to a city; Donald could see it in the distance. There were some tall buildings with tile roofs that turned up at the corners. There were houses with walled gardens. There were temples with carved ornaments covered with gold. In the center of the city was a big open space.

Wingman flew low and circled over the open space. It was a market. It reminded Donald of Chinatown. People were buying and selling groceries. Boys were helping their fathers carry baskets of vegetables, eggs, meat. Donald could hear them talking. He could smell things cooking, shu-mai and wonton. It made him hungry. There was a little boy eating what looked like a lotus root cake while he waited for his father, who talked with friends. It was like Chinatown, but bigger, sunnier, happier. Donald wished Wingman would put him down. He wanted

to talk to the boy with the lotus root cake. He wanted to walk among the grocers' stalls. He wanted to smell up close all the things cooking. He had the feeling that he would meet Oi-Lai Bok selling newspapers and comics in Chinese. Then someone saw them. There was a shout, and Wingman flapped his wings hard. They rose straight up, into the cold air. The city fell away so fast that Donald had a funny feeling in his stomach.

They flew over farms again, and hills. They were getting into a place where there were lots of hills. Some of them were very high, mountains almost. At times the peaks were as high as the tips of Wingman's wings.

Some people were moving on a path, two men and a boy. They were leading a horse. They were high up, close to Donald and Wingman, and Donald could see their faces clearly. One of the men looked a lot like his uncle, Li-Noon, except that instead of an overcoat and a gray felt hat, this Li-Noon wore a long cloak of a beautiful blue color.

It came almost to the ground, and at the bottom showed a little of another robe that the man had on underneath. It reminded Donald of the robe his mother used to wear in the mornings, before she had left them for the hospital. Then they had passed over them and they were out of sight before Donald had seen all he wanted to see of the man who looked like Uncle Noon.

It was getting foggy. The hills were real mountains now. Wingman landed Donald on a little bridge that connected two rocky cliff faces. A long way down, below the little bridge, there was a stream. Wingman stood on the bridge and flapped his wings twice. Then they became soft, and fell about his shoulders and were his cape of feathers again. He sat down on the bridge, his feet dangling over the side, and Donald sat down too.

He looked down at the river and heard a faint rushing noise. The noise got louder and louder as the fog closed in. It was getting cold, and late; the traffic overhead was getting heavier. Donald was back on the George Washington Bridge. Wingman was gone.

He was holding something in his hand. It was a gray feather. It could almost have been a pigeon feather, but Donald recognized it as one of the feathers from Wingman's cape. He put it in his pocket.

Getting down from the icy bridge was not easy. Donald could not climb down the way he usually did. He had to slide down the slanting girders, or push himself along with his hands until he came to a place where he could drop to a lower level. He was constantly slipping and the ice hurt his hands.

The only way to get down the big wall part at the bottom was to slide down. When it wasn't icy he could slide down slowly by dragging the rubber toes of his basketball shoes against the concrete, and sort of hugging it with his body and the palms of his hands. This time he just slid down like a brick. It was almost like falling straight down for ten or twelve feet.

When he hit the bottom, it knocked the wind out of him and he couldn't move for a minute or two. The first thing he did when he could move his hand was to reach in his pocket and see if the feather was there. He hadn't been afraid at all.

Donald got home too late to help his father. It was already time for supper. He was very hungry. There was soup, and chicken in soy sauce, vegetables, hot tea, and lotus root cakes for dessert. Donald ate three cakes.

"In China," his father said, "those used to taste even better."

"I thought so," Donald said.

Donald had some Little Lulu comics that he kept to trade with. That night he made a deal with his sister. She got the Little Lulus, and Donald got her box of crayons.

When his sister and brother had gone to sleep, Donald began to draw in a Big Chief pencil tablet. He wanted to make a picture of everything he had seen in China. He began a picture of fields and hills, and worked on it

until he was sleepy. He put the crayons and the tablet under his mattress, where no one would find them. He put Wingman's feather there too.

During the night it snowed and rained and froze. In the morning the street was slick with ice. Cars and buses were slowly skidding sideways, and people were walking with tiny baby steps to keep from slipping. When Donald got to the little park, every tree was covered with ice. Even the tiniest twigs had a shining clear skin. The bridge was covered with ice too. Donald saw that there was no way he could climb it. He looked for Wingman and the eagle, but he could not see them.

The rest of the vacation was icy. When it wasn't icy, it was raining and snowing. There wasn't one day when it would have been possible for Donald to climb the bridge. He helped his father, spent time getting his comic book collection in order, and worked on the pictures of China in the Big Chief pencil tablet. One day Donald and some other kids slid down St. Nicholas Avenue on sleds made out of cardboard boxes. On Christmas Eve the family had a special supper. The best part was hot dumplings filled with minced pork, and dipped in plum sauce. Donald got a sweater from his father.

On Christmas Day the children stayed home, and their father took the train to visit their mother. Children were not allowed in the hospital. Donald had to take care of his brother and sister and fix their lunch. They were very quiet. It was raining outside. Donald read a lot of comics. There was Christmas music playing on the radio.

All of a sudden it was time for school to start again. It took Donald by surprise. The vacation had not worked out the way he had planned. He had hoped every day that he would be able to climb the bridge again. His notebook was almost full of pictures, and he wanted to fly with Wingman. He wanted to go to China, and now he would have to go to Public School 132.

He knew there was no way to get out of it. He had promised his father not to cut school again. When he woke up in the morning he hoped he was sick. He kept his eyes shut for at least five minutes and tried to make himself have a fever. It didn't work; he didn't feel sick; he just felt miserable.

He went to school. He didn't expect things to be different from the way they had been. He was wrong. When he got to his classroom, Miss Spinrad was not there! At Miss Spinrad's desk was a little woman with red hair and eyeglasses. She was younger than Miss Spinrad, and there was something strange about her face. Donald couldn't figure out exactly what it was. Maybe it was because she was a little person; she almost seemed like one of the kids. Maybe it was because she looked human; Miss Spinrad looked like Frankenstein. Whatever it was, the other kids had noticed it too, because they were sitting quietly at their desks. That wasn't the way they usually acted with a substitute teacher.

"My name is Mrs. Miller," she said. "Miss

Spinrad is sick, and will not be back this term. I will be your teacher."

"Yaaay," the kids shouted.

Mrs. Miller acted as though she thought school was supposed to be fun. None of the teachers Donald had ever had, and certainly not Miss Spinrad, had ever acted that way. At first it was confusing for Donald and the other kids. Mrs. Miller would do weird things, like asking the class what they felt like studying. And smiling at them.

She wanted to hear people read all the time. When Miss Spinrad had the kids read out loud, she would hold a little notebook in her hand. If someone made a mistake or got confused, she would smile to herself and write something in the notebook. She seemed to like it when kids got mixed up. She would always say, "You are the worst readers in the worst school in New York."

It was true that most of the kids in the class couldn't read very well, but they found that it was a lot easier to read for Mrs. Miller.

She really wanted to hear them read, and she never left a kid choking on a word he couldn't figure out. She always helped.

It turned out that Donald was the best reader in the class. Mrs. Miller asked him what he liked to read.

"Comics," he told her.

Mrs. Miller asked him if he owned a lot of comics.

"About two thousand," Donald said.

"Would you like to bring some to school?" Mrs. Miller asked.

Donald couldn't believe it. Every time he had been caught with a comic book in school, it had meant a visit to Mr. Frieda, who always tore them up.

For part of every day, when the other kids worked on reading, Donald was allowed to sit at the back of the room, reading comics. As some of the other kids got better at reading, they were allowed to join Donald and read comics with him, and Donald was supposed to help them. Every day he brought twenty or thirty comics to school with him. All the kids wanted to join the group that got time off to read comics, so they all tried to get better at reading. At lunch, the kids who got to read the comics would sit together and talk about the stories.

Donald knew more about comics than anybody, and he was always in the center of the group. A couple of the other kids started collecting. Donald gave away some doubles, and sometimes he and the other kids would trade comics after school.

Wingman wasn't around any more. Donald had looked for him on the bridge, but he was never there. After a while, Donald stopped looking for him. On weekends he would hang out with some kids from his class, going to bookstores that sold secondhand comics, or just fooling around. One day he paid a nickel for a perfect copy of *Action Comics Number 1*, which had the first Superman story ever. He felt good about that because now he had every number.

Donald's whole class got to read comics,

and after a while Mrs. Miller said that since they could read comics at home, it might be a good idea to quit reading them in school. Some of the kids complained, but Mrs. Miller said she would get them some good books to read instead. Donald had already decided that he liked comics better outside of school. Reading comics in class was fun at first, but in some way reading them there made it sort of official, and took some of the fun away.

Mrs. Miller had thought of something to take the place of the comics. On the same day she told the class that she had arranged for them to take some trips. That was *really* special. None of the kids had ever heard of a class taking a trip, certainly not a class from P.S. 132.

Mrs. Miller spoke to the kids about how she wanted them to behave on the trip, and told them to bring subway fare and their lunches, and to meet her outside of the school on the following Wednesday because they were going to spend the whole day at the Metropolitan Museum of Art. They were going on a trip!

They were going on the subway! They weren't even going *inside* the school! Everybody wished it was Wednesday.

For the next few days Mrs. Miller talked to the class about the museum, and the things they would see. None of the kids had ever been to a museum, and she wanted to prepare them for it.

None of them was prepared for how big it was. It was ten times as big as the school! The class stood lined up in twos outside the museum, at the bottom of the biggest, widest steps in the world.

"Follow me, class," Mrs. Miller said, and the children toiled up the steps after her.

The class passed through a huge door into the biggest room anyone had ever seen. Their feet made clicking noises on the smooth floor, and there was an echo. Everybody tried out the echo by whistling and shouting, until Mrs. Miller reminded them that they were guests, and the museum people liked things quiet.

Donald had read stories in comics about museums; Batman was always catching crooks who were trying to steal a famous diamond or a gold statue from one. But this was real! There were real suits of armor, and old axes, swords, and spears. This was in a room hung with beautiful flags, and in the middle there was a dummy knight in real armor on a dummy horse. The horse had armor too. Mrs. Miller talked about the armor, and the people who had used it. The kids could almost hear the crashing and banging as soldiers fought with swords and shields.

Mrs. Miller led the class through a dark stone passage into a room that was arranged to look like an Egyptian tomb. There were mummies, and big stone statues of cats and birds. It was scary. Mrs. Miller talked about how old the things in that room were, thousands and thousands of years! She told them about life in ancient Egypt and about the tombs and mummies. The class was very quiet. Most of them had seen a movie about a mummy in a museum who comes to life.

The boys whispered dares to each other to come back to the mummy room alone.

The museum was so full of wonderful things that it was hard to take. By the time the class went down to the basement to eat their lunches in a special room there, a lot of kids had blown their tops. It was just too much to see. It was too exciting. In their minds the kids were knights on horseback and mummies come to life. They were thrilled by pictures full of sunlight; they were full of sunlight too. They needed a chance to let off steam. It was a loud lunch.

After lunch the class went upstairs to look at the Chinese paintings. Donald was waiting for that. He had never heard about Chinese paintings until Mrs. Miller began telling her class about the things they would see in the museum. Donald had a special reason for wanting to see pictures of China.

The room was small, and the pictures, hung side by side, were painted on silk. They were not filled with sunlight like some of the paintings they had seen earlier; they were filled with mist and empty spaces. The class was quiet looking at the pictures, not because they were scary like the Egyptian things, but because there was something about these pictures that was like a little bird perched on your finger. If you were to make a sudden move, or even breathe, the bird might get frightened and fly away.

"These are not paintings of light; they are pictures of moments in time," Mrs. Miller was saying. The class was hardly listening to her; they could see that for themselves.

Donald was searching for something in the paintings. He had seen mountains like this, and the same kind of little houses before. He was looking for a landmark, for something he had seen for sure that day he had flown over China. He found it. In a picture of trees and mountains and swirling fog, there were three tiny figures, two men and a boy. They were leading a horse. One of the men looked a lot like his uncle, Li-Noon.

Donald felt a rushing in his ears. He could

hear the traffic on the George Washington Bridge. He could smell the trees in the misty mountain forest. He felt suspended in the air, as though Wingman were carrying him. He must have looked funny, because Mrs. Miller put her hand on his shoulder as she talked to the class about the picture. He felt her hand and the rushing went away. "Perhaps some ancestor of Donald Chen painted this picture, or maybe one of the people in the picture is Donald as he would have been in China nine hundred years ago."

She had made an awfully good guess. Donald wanted to say something to Mrs. Miller, but he was too confused and excited to speak. The class was about to move on to another room, when Donald found his voice. "I want to stay here."

Mrs. Miller told Donald he could stay with the Chinese paintings if he would promise not to leave the room; then she could find him when it was time to go home. Donald promised and the class filed out.

Donald was alone with the picture. There was something more he wanted to see in it. He studied the picture inch by inch. He looked at the leafy trees; he looked at the curious shapes of mountains. He looked at the three figures leading the horse. The horse was white. It had a beautiful silk cloth covering its back. Donald wondered why none of them rode the horse. He looked into the mist, the empty spaces. There was something else he wanted the picture to show him.

Then the mist began to move. It stopped being flat. It stopped being a picture. The painting was turning into a window. The people were real. Donald felt a cool breeze. He could also feel the heat of the horse's body. Then it was flat again, a picture again. There was a little bench in the room, in front of the painting, and Donald went and sat down on it. He tried to make the painting turn into a window again. It stayed flat. Donald got tired of trying and just sat, gazing in the direction of the picture, thinking about nothing. The mist started swirling. "Hey! It's real again!" he thought. The picture went flat that moment.

Donald discovered that he could play a game with the painting. As long as he looked at it, just looked without thinking or paying attention to anything in particular, the picture was real. It was alive. It moved. But, if he thought about any one thing, a part of the picture, Donald Chen, the bench, the room, anything, the picture went flat, was just a picture again. It was like watching something out of the corner of his eye, only he was looking right at it.

Donald played the game; soon he was getting better at it. At first he could only make the picture real for maybe a second at a time. After practicing, he was able to make it real for as long as he wanted. Then he discovered that he could think about separate things in the picture, but if he thought about himself thinking, it would all go flat again and he would have to start over.

Donald had known from the first that what he wanted was to make Wingman appear in the picture. Now he thought that maybe Wingman would only appear if he did not think about him. Donald discovered that it was very hard to keep from thinking of something once he knew what the something was. He kept trying.

He made some progress. He knew just where in the empty space Wingman would appear, but each time he tried, just before he

would have been able to see him, he couldn't help thinking, "I can almost see him!" and the painting would go flat.

"Donald, the class is ready to leave." Mrs. Miller had come to get him. As they left the room, Donald glanced back at the painting. Wingman was flying over the mountains.

Donald wanted to tell Mrs. Miller what had happened, what he had seen in the picture. He wanted to know if other people saw things in pictures that way. He wanted to tell her about Wingman, and flying to China. In his mind he practiced different ways to tell her. None of the ways seemed right. He rode the subway and went home without saying anything. That night he couldn't get to sleep. All the things that happened kept popping up in his mind. It was bothering him. He had to think of a way to let somebody else know. He wanted it to be Mrs. Miller. She had been the one to take him to the museum. She knew about pictures.

At the same time, Donald knew that he

couldn't just tell her that someone who was like a hero in a comic book had appeared to him eight stories up in the steel girders of the George Washington Bridge, had a pet eagle, took Donald flying, not just to China, but to China a thousand years ago. You can't tell anybody things like that. Donald knew that it would be a bad mistake even to tell anyone that he had climbed the bridge.

He had to think of a way of telling her without letting her know that she had been told. He thought of a way to do it, just as he fell asleep. He dreamed the sort of dreams he always did, dreams in the shape of comic book stories, brightly colored panels one after another. In the morning, he didn't know if he had dreamed it, or thought of it, or planned to do it all along. He took his notebook, the one with all his drawings, from under his mattress and put it in his schoolbag.

At the end of the day, Donald handed the notebook to Mrs. Miller and went home. He felt good; now someone else knew. When he got home his father was ironing sheets, and Donald thought about how much he liked the sweet, steamy, laundry smells. He was learning to cook. His father had left bok choy and onions and mushrooms for Donald to cut up. Later they cooked some chicken in the big bowl-shaped frying pan, poured in the vegetables Donald had cut, and served supper to the little kids.

At school the next day, Mrs. Miller asked Donald to stay after school. His friends thought he was going to be punished for something. They said they would wait for him outside, but Donald knew that she was going to say something about his pictures. He liked her for not talking about them in front of the class. Mrs. Miller never embarrassed people.

"Thank you, Donald, for letting me see these fine pictures," she said. "Have you been drawing for a long time?"

Donald mumbled something. He was a little embarrassed after all.

"You know, most schools have Art as a regular subject, but this school . . . well, this school doesn't. However, I went to the supply room and found these." Mrs. Miller went to the cabinet. She took out a roll of big sheets of paper, yellowish and rough, and nearly as big as Donald himself when she unrolled them. She rolled them up again and handed them to Donald. She also gave him a box containing little jars of color and a brush.

"Since no one uses these things, I don't see why you shouldn't have them," Mrs. Miller said. Donald was really embarrassed now. He was mumbling again.

"There is something you can do for me," Mrs. Miller said. "Will you do a very good picture on one of these sheets of paper, and bring it to me? I will give it back to you after a while."

"Sure," Donald said. "That's okay." He was talking like a dumb jerk; he wanted to kick himself. He felt like crying or hugging Mrs. Miller. He took the paper and the box of paints and left, running.

Donald had to get his father's help. The paper was too big to keep under the mattress. They arranged that Donald would cover the ironing table with newspaper in the evening, and do his painting there. His brother and sister were ordered to keep their hands off the painting stuff.

His father was very excited about the project. The first night Donald tried to paint, he kept looking over Donald's shoulder to see how it was coming. Donald messed up a couple of sheets of paper just getting used to the paint. His father watched him. Every time he brushed a new color onto the paper, his father clapped and laughed as though he were watching fireworks. Donald started to laugh too, and they wound up laughing until their eyes were wet, especially his father's.

Donald started to work on a serious paint-ing the next night. He decided to paint the marketplace in the old Chinese city he had seen. He also put a dragon in the picture. He had seen a dragon in New York City just a few days before, in Chinatown with his father, brother, and sister. It was New Year's—not January first, but Chinese New Year, which comes later—and he had seen a dragon dancing in the street. It was not really a dragon, but a lot of people dressed up as a dragon. Donald could see their feet. It was a little like a giant caterpillar. There were firecrackers going off everywhere, and the people inside made the dragon twist and turn and rear his head up in the air. Donald liked it a lot.

Donald painted the dragon dancing in the open square. He painted the buildings, and the vegetable stalls. He painted crowds of people watching the dragon; he made some of them look like people he knew. His father was carrying a stack of sheets; Uncle Noon had a big bottle of wine. He painted his brother and sister, and the three people from the picture in the museum, leading their horse. He painted exploding firecrackers the way they are shown in comic books, two red halves with a yellow flash between them. For good measure, he painted some up-in-the-sky fireworks. Above it all, very small, he painted Wingman and himself, flying in a corner of the sky.

When the picture was finished, he signed it, Chen Chi-Wing. His father put it in the window of the laundry on Saturday. All day long people came in to say nice things about the picture. Donald kept going out in the street to look at it. It was a pretty good picture, there was no doubt about it.

On Monday he took the picture to Mrs. Miller. He told her she could keep it, but she said she would keep it just for a while. When school was over that day, he saw her take the rolled-up picture out of the cabinet and take it with her.

Time passed in the ordinary way. Donald had some of the big sheets of paper left, and did some more pictures. He found a rare comic he had been looking for, *Barney Baxter Four Color Number 20*. He also made a couple of visits to the museum on his own. He was getting better at the game of letting the picture come to life, and he also tried it on different kinds of pictures. With some it worked, with some it didn't. In school they were learning about the Indians who used to live right in his neighborhood before New York City was there. He liked that pretty well, and kept up with his homework. He hadn't cut school or climbed the bridge for a long time.

So he was not prepared for the note Mrs. Miller gave him to take home. It said that the principal of P.S. 132 invited Donald and his father to meet him in his office the next morning. Mrs. Miller had said that she hoped it would be a pleasant surprise. Donald tried to remember if he ever heard of anything pleasant happening in the principal's office. He hadn't, so he spent some time trying to remember some crime for which he had not been caught.

In the morning he still had no idea what the principal had found out. His father was wearing his suit. He didn't say anything one way or the other. They went to school together.

In the hall outside the principal's office, there was a big glass case, almost as big as a store window. There was a fluorescent light inside it, but the light was always out. Donald had never seen anything on display in the case. This morning the light was on, and in the case, tacked to a big sheet of red construction paper, was Donald's painting, the one he had given to Mrs. Miller.

Donald and his father began to smile. Mrs. Miller saw them through the open door of the office, and she and the principal, Mr. Toomey, came out into the hall. They both shook hands with Donald's father, and Mr. Toomey shook hands with Donald. He called him Don.

Mrs. Miller explained that she had entered Donald's picture in a city-wide school art contest. One hundred and nineteen schools had each sent a picture by one of the pupils, and Donald's picture had been selected as the best of the hundred and nineteen.

Mr. Toomey shook hands with Donald again, and gave him his prize, which consisted of a blue ribbon, a sheet of paper with fancy writing on it saying Donald had won the contest, and a five-dollar bill. Donald's father kept patting him on the back and saying, "Good boy." Donald gave his father the prizes to take home.

Mrs. Miller told the class that they could see Donald's picture outside the principal's office. "Also," she said, "Mr. Toomey has decided that we should have Art as a regular subject, so, starting next week, we will paint pictures on Tuesday and Thursday afternoons." After the cheering died down, the class settled to work on the old-time Indians of Manhattan.

Donald was looking out the window. Nobody else saw the bird, or if they did, they thought it was a pigeon and hardly looked at it. Donald watched the eagle glide and spiral higher and higher. Even after it was out of sight he heard its shrill cries.

ABOUT THE AUTHOR

DANIEL PINKWATER is the author of more than fifty books for children and young adults. He is heard regularly as a commentator on National Public Radio's program, "All Things Considered." He is the author of the other Bantam Skylark titles *The Muffin Fiend* and *Lizard Music*. Mr. Pinkwater lives on a small farm in upstate New York with his wife, Jill Pinkwater.